Dear Parents and Educators,

Welcome to Penguin Young Readers! As parent
know that each child develops at his or her own pace—in terms of
speech, critical thinking, and, of course, reading. Penguin Young
Readers recognizes this fact. As a result, each Penguin Young Readers
book is assigned a traditional easy-to-read level (1–4) as well as a
Guided Reading Level (A–P). Both of these systems will help you
choose the right book for your child. Please refer to the back of each
book for specific leveling information. Penguin Young Readers features
esteemed authors and illustrators, stories about favorite characters,
fascinating nonfiction, and more!

Clara and Clem Take a Ride

LEVEL 1

GUIDED
READING
LEVEL **C**

This book is perfect for an **Emergent Reader** who:
- can read in a left-to-right and top-to-bottom progression;
- can recognize some beginning and ending letter sounds;
- can use picture clues to help tell the story; and
- can understand the basic plot and sequence of simple stories.

Here are some **activities** you can do during and after reading this book:
- Picture Clues: Use the pictures in this book to tell the story. Go through
  the book, retelling the story just by looking at the pictures.
- Sight Words: Sight words are frequently used words that readers
  must know just by looking at them. They are known instantly, on sight.
  Knowing these words helps children develop into efficient readers. As
  you read the story, have the child point out the sight words below.

a	go	look	see	to
come	in	me	stop	with

Remember, sharing the love of reading with a child is the best gift
you can give!

—Bonnie Bader, EdM
   Penguin Young Readers program

*Penguin Young Readers are leveled by independent reviewers applying the standards developed by Irene Fountas
and Gay Su Pinnell in *Matching Books to Readers: Using Leveled Books in Guided Reading*, Heinemann, 1999.

To my wife, Heather, who creates new
adventures for us every day—EL

Penguin Young Readers
Published by the Penguin Group
Penguin Group (USA) Inc., 375 Hudson Street, New York, New York 10014, USA
Penguin Group (Canada), 90 Eglinton Avenue East, Suite 700, Toronto, Ontario M4P 2Y3, Canada
(a division of Pearson Penguin Canada Inc.)
Penguin Books Ltd., 80 Strand, London WC2R 0RL, England
Penguin Group Ireland, 25 St. Stephen's Green, Dublin 2, Ireland
(a division of Penguin Books Ltd.)
Penguin Group (Australia), 250 Camberwell Road, Camberwell, Victoria 3124, Australia
(a division of Pearson Australia Group Pty. Ltd.)
Penguin Books India Pvt. Ltd., 11 Community Centre, Panchsheel Park, New Delhi—110 017, India
Penguin Group (NZ), 67 Apollo Drive, Rosedale, Auckland 0632, New Zealand
(a division of Pearson New Zealand Ltd.)
Penguin Books (South Africa) (Pty.) Ltd., 24 Sturdee Avenue,
Rosebank, Johannesburg 2196, South Africa

Penguin Books Ltd., Registered Offices: 80 Strand, London WC2R 0RL, England

Library of Congress Cataloging-in-Publication Data is available.

ISBN 978-0-448-46264-6 (pbk)   10 9 8 7 6 5 4 3 2 1
ISBN 978-0-448-46271-4 (hc)   10 9 8 7 6 5 4 3 2 1

PENGUIN YOUNG READERS

LEVEL 1

EMERGENT READER

Clara and CLEM Take a Ride

by Ethan Long

Penguin Young Readers
An Imprint of Penguin Group (USA) Inc.

5

6

There's the sun.

That's The End.